# SPINE-CHILLERS

## HAUNTED TALES

Edited By Jenni Harrison

**Years of** YoungWriters

First published in Great Britain in 2020 by:

Est. 1991

Young Writers
Remus House
Coltsfoot Drive
Peterborough
PE2 9BF
Telephone: 01733 890066
Website: www.youngwriters.co.uk

Printed and bound in the UK by BookPrintingUK
Website: www.bookprintinguk.com
YB0451EZ

# FOREWORD

Enter, Reader, if you dare...

For as long as there have been stories there have been ghost stories. Writers have been trying scare their readers for centuries using just the power of their imagination. For Young Writers' latest competition Spine-Chillers we asked pupils to come up with their own spooky tales, but with the tricky twist of using just 100 words!

They rose to the challenge magnificently and this resulting collection of haunting tales will certainly give you the creeps! From friendly ghosts and Halloween adventures to the gruesome and macabre, the young writers in this anthology showcase their creative writing talents.

Here at Young Writers our aim is to encourage creativity and to inspire a love of the written word, so it's great to get such an amazing response, with some absolutely fantastic stories.

I'd like to congratulate all the young authors in this collection - I hope this inspires them to continue with their creative writing. And who knows, maybe we'll be seeing their names alongside Stephen King on the best seller lists in the future...

# CONTENTS

## ALL SAINTS CATHOLIC HIGH SCHOOL, SHEFFIELD

Rachael Hanson (15) — 1
Ritchie Junior Claravall (12) — 2

## ARC SCHOOL OLD ARLEY, ANSLEY

Zack Clarke (12) — 3

## CHESSBROOK EDUCATION SUPPORT CENTRE, WATFORD

Ritchie Nash (14) — 4
Kai Savage (16) — 5

## EBBW FAWR LEANING COMMUNITY - SECOND PHASE, EBBW VALE

Kasia Tomsa (14) — 6

## HAYWOOD ACADEMY, BURSLEM

Elizabeth Bailey (13) — 7
Anna Coates (15) — 8
Kirsten Else (14) — 9
Chloe Cotterill (14) — 10
George Thomas Bentley (15) — 11
Charlotte Pursey (15) — 12
Elisha Louise Hall (15) — 13
Benjamin Ware (14) — 14
Chloe Rhodes (14) — 15
Carlos Marchese (12) — 16
Nusrat Leeton (13) — 17

Keira Stamp (14) — 18
Emma Williams (14) — 19
Usaam Arfan (12) — 20
Suhayla Bint-Ahmed (15) — 21
Zoe Jackson (14) — 22
Kady Povey (11) — 23
Louisa Durber (15) — 24
Charis Hargreaves (13) — 25
Grace Shepherd (15) — 26
Jessica Jolley (12) — 27
Lucy Osborne (12) — 28
Jack Mills (15) — 29
Cheyenne Kime-Lawton (13) — 30
Jessica Paige Spicer (12) — 31
Sam Beattie (14) — 32
Lewis Maxfield (11) — 33
Mia Howard (13) — 34
Zonaira Akbar (12) — 35
Vinaz Maran Sadik (14) — 36
Ollie Martin (12) — 37
Lucy Glover (12) — 38
Lauren Guderis (14) — 39

## MILLFIELD PREPARATORY SCHOOL, GLASTONBURY

Dexter Townsend (11) — 40
Eva Lawson (12) — 41
Daniel Pearce (12) — 42
Daniel Blight (12) — 43
Tilly Anderton (12) — 44

## NORTHFLEET TECHNOLOGY COLLEGE, NORTHFLEET

Borys Stachowicz — 45
Garry Cunningham (15) — 46

## Oakgrove School, Middleton

| | |
|---|---|
| Janelle Allison (12) | 47 |
| Natasha Yallop (14) | 48 |

## Ormiston Denes Academy, Lowestoft

| | |
|---|---|
| Damion Knibbs (13) | 49 |
| Mia Mirgaux (13) | 50 |
| Bethany Hannant (12) | 51 |

## Outwood Academy Danum, Doncaster

| | |
|---|---|
| Thomas Annakin (11) | 52 |
| Scarlett Byrne (13) | 53 |
| Hannah Roberts (13) | 54 |
| Aymaan Khurram (14) | 55 |
| Jessica Noorany (12) | 56 |
| Poppy Reardon (14) | 57 |
| Scarlett Rollinson (14) | 58 |
| Ellison Smith (14) | 59 |
| William Bates (12) | 60 |
| Jakub Kowalewski (13) | 61 |
| Georgiana Ungureanu (13) | 62 |
| Owen Bunday (11) | 63 |
| Ioana Gongeanu (11) | 64 |
| Jack Brookes (12) | 65 |
| Beliz Erdogdu (13) | 66 |
| Hayden Horne (12) | 67 |

## Ramsey Grammar School, Isle Of Man

| | |
|---|---|
| Abbie Dixon | 68 |

## Scalby School, Newby

| | |
|---|---|
| Mirren Elwick (12) | 69 |
| Louis Fell (12) | 70 |
| Evie Wardell (15) | 71 |
| Zachary Parker (12) | 72 |
| Emily Gaskell (11) | 73 |
| Kaitlyn Jayde Byram (12) | 74 |

| | |
|---|---|
| Kyle Robinson (12) | 75 |
| Hannah Brown (12) | 76 |
| Harrison Roebuck (13) | 77 |
| Isobel Pashby (14) | 78 |
| Amelie Williams (12) | 79 |
| Hannah Sellers-Drury (14) | 80 |
| Marylynn Rodger (15) | 81 |
| Matilda Brown (13) | 82 |
| Jack Langmead (14) | 83 |
| Rose Wanless (12) | 84 |
| Lucy Brown (12) | 85 |
| Harriet Benson (12) | 86 |
| Stan Vickers (12) | 87 |
| Thomas Jey (12) | 88 |
| Jack Parkes (13) | 89 |
| Liana More (12) | 90 |
| Ellis Mearns (13) | 91 |
| Alfie Race (13) | 92 |
| Charlie Broadhead (13) | 93 |
| Aidan Stockill (14) | 94 |

## Solefield School, Sevenoaks

| | |
|---|---|
| Christopher Horn (10) | 95 |
| Joshua Edwards (12) | 96 |
| Luke Edwards (12) | 97 |
| Kinn Jansen (11) | 98 |
| Arthur Mitchell-Clark (11) | 99 |
| William Walters (11) | 100 |
| Harry Paterson (12) | 101 |
| Finlay Hawkins | 102 |
| George Brown | 103 |
| Jasper Tym | 104 |

## St Andrew The Apostle Greek Orthodox School, London

| | |
|---|---|
| Kristian Michael (15) | 105 |
| Ben Reid (15) | 106 |
| Jason Marvon (14) | 107 |
| Mia Lo Bue (14) | 108 |
| Sienna Tierney (11) | 109 |
| Anna Photiou (13) | 110 |

## St Catherine's College, Eastbourne

Lois Katie Hilton (15)        111

## St Thomas More RC Academy, North Shields

Michaela Redpath (12)        112
Izzy Dutton (13)        113
Grace Peddie (13)        114

## The Literacy House International, Tintagel

Teerna Bhaumik (11)        115
Samara Noronha (12)        116

## The Portsmouth Academy, Portsmouth

Lois Van Den Broek (13)        117
Oakley Lancett (13)        118
Brooke Knight (12)        119
Jannah Bushra (12)        120
Charlie Payne        121

# THE MINI SAGAS

# ENDLESS STAIRCASE

The door swung open and he stepped in with a torch in hand. It flickered into life and revealed the staircase before home, infinite darkness - according to the foundation. Breathing heavily, he began his way down, slowly making sure he didn't slip and fall. Every flight of stairs brought on something new: cracks, locked doors, and numerous other possibilities. He reached floor 36 when noise could be heard behind him, almost a deep growl-like noise. Hurrying forward slightly, he stared back, not looking ahead of himself. A major mistake. His back now against a wall, the darkness took shape.

RACHAEL HANSON (15)
All Saints Catholic High School, Sheffield

# THE REAPER'S LEVIATHAN

It's been weeks since the crash, the ocean is a big place, I can't even see the wreck. Last night I couldn't sleep. I heard a rumbling beneath me, a muffled croak, even now in the daylight I can see a shadow, night's coming. I've never seen one like the one last night, it was a devil, a fish serpent that came from Hell. It was red and white with a Reaper's scythe on its head, its eyes were black, no pupils, its tail long, the tell-tale of a Leviathan, the Reaper's Leviathan.

## RITCHIE JUNIOR CLARAVALL (12)

All Saints Catholic High School, Sheffield

# THE SCREAM

The room was dark and silent, the only noise was my own breathing or was it someone else's? My heart was beating heavily I knew it wanted to jump out and run away but I needed the company. The door slammed shut! I could hear footsteps progressing towards me. My eyes started to water, I started to sweat and then I did something I regret. I screamed but nobody could hear it over the clattering sound of the chainsaw brushing against my arm. The blood dripped down and splashed on the ground I punched at the figure's legs and ran...

ZACK CLARKE (12)

Arc School Old Arley, Ansley

# ABANDONED HAUNTED SCHOOL

As we broke into the boarded-up school, we heard a faint bell ringing in the distance. We thought we'd just hit something, but then it happened again. We nervously crept towards it until we discovered it. It stopped ringing immediately. A faded shadow of a person was stood against the wall by the bell. It knew we were there. It turned. Red eyes glared at us. Its sharp teeth were dripping with blood. The shadow looked hungry for another victim. Making eye-to-eye contact, it slowly slithered towards us with a high-pitched, deafening screech.

RITCHIE NASH (14)

Chessbrook Education Support Centre, Watford

# TRAPPED IN THE ENDLESS CORNFIELDS

Running endlessly towards the screams and cries of help for whom I'd entered with, I seemed to get closer but the heart-wrenching screeches appeared to have been thrown in the opposite direction. "What is happening?" I stopped running. I felt hopeless and alone. Suddenly, I awaken to the sound of my friend calling for me. Rising up to my feet slowly, I'm lost and confused. I'm so close to her voice it hasn't run away from me this time. I etch slowly forward to a part of the field that has been cut and I see it...

KAI SAVAGE (16)

Chessbrook Education Support Centre, Watford

# THE UNKNOWN BEYOND...

Unwillingly the distraught path seemed to grasp me closer. The silent cries of desperation filled the rancid air that choked my throat. Like a blossoming flower in a field of decay, the illuminated and silver gate beckoned me towards it but what lay beyond was not so inviting. It was a nightmare. The alarmingly cold bite of the wind nipped at my shivering arms as my hand trembled in the darkness. I was trapped. That was until the horror blinded me with memory. I always knew I had a connection to this horrid and dreaded place. Now I knew why.

## KASIA TOMSA (14)

Ebbw Fawr Leaning Community - Second Phase, Ebbw Vale

# THE HOUSE NEXT DOOR

There was this house next door that looked abandoned. It had windows that looked like eyes and the door looked like a mouth to a beast. We went in, there was lots of dust and spiderwebs everywhere. "Boo!"

"Argh!"

"Don't do that!" After that, we went upstairs, it felt like someone was watching us.

"I-is t-that pict-ture watching us?"

"Run!" We went into the bedroom...

"Boo"

"Don't start that again!"

"That wasn't me!"

"Ghost, run!" We went downstairs.

"Did you hear that?"

"Yes."

"Argghhhh!"

Missing report: two children went missing yesterday, the police are still looking today.

ELIZABETH BAILEY (13)
Haywood Academy, Burslem

# CONTROL

Darkness seeps into the manor as Stevenson sits bewitched by his reflection. Staring despondently into the eyes of a monster. The personification of his deepest desires.The need of someone's life in his hands. Screams echoing through the manor, bouncing off each blood-splattered wall. All morals long-gone. Hostage to this repressed persona. He attempts to cover his tracks as the thoughts only grow stronger. The monster in the mirror cannot be restrained. Stevenson's barely there anymore, wholly replaced by the blood-lusting personality. All attempts to wrangle back control were fruitless. Only death would take his guilt and desires away.

ANNA COATES (15)
Haywood Academy, Burslem

# HUNTED

In a dark bedroom, a girl bolted up, her eyes widening with panic. A laugh rang out, ringing through her being. "You remember how to play my game?" The girl stood up trembling. "You know the goal. Escape!" His playful tone hardened. "I'm coming..."

The girl ran out into a maze.

"Where are you?" The voice sang from her left. She raced away, praying. The

walls blurred together. Then she tripped. The knife was suddenly pressed

against her. "30 seconds." Her eyes closed, waiting for the inevitable.

Her eyes opened to see her hunter twirling a crimson blade. "Round 10?"

## KIRSTEN ELSE (14)

Haywood Academy, Burslem

# Hidden Noises

We started to walk through the wood, which was dark and so dense we couldn't see what was in front of us. The trees loomed above us. I started to imagine that the trees' branches were their arms and they were going to snatch us as we walked past. I started to hear strange, mysterious noises as my heart began pounding with fear. "What's that?" I exclaimed, terrified.

Layla looked at me. "I'm scared!" she cried.

I heard branches crunching behind me, something started to shake me. I screamed out.

"Wake up Chloe!" soothed Mum. "You're having a bad dream."

## Chloe Cotterill (14)

Haywood Academy, Burslem

# FADING

The narrow windows impeded any light from entering, dust particles surrounded them as they venture slowly into the room. Each room scarier, creepier and darker than the last. Impaled by light, all visions lost they must keep going. Navigating through the doorway, light illuminating their panic-stricken faces. The light fades to dim. This room was a child's. Bright colours, cute toys. The light keeps fading, the rocking horse sits quietly in the corner. *Crash!* All light has gone, all life has gone, the rumble lies still from the balcony above. The rocking horse rocks in the dark!

## GEORGE THOMAS BENTLEY (15)

Haywood Academy, Burslem

# HIDE-AND-SEEK

I raced around the corner, glancing back at the figures that were so eagerly pursuing me. Spying out an oak door, I swiftly reached out for the handle, scraping at it in a panic to get it open. I clambered inside, tugging the door shut behind me. Cryptic silhouettes surrounded my figure, waiting and watching. I overheard footsteps and muffled giggles outside, accompanied by a raucous creak as the door was swung open. Three people stood above me, shouting the dreaded words, "We found you!" I peered back at the closet, it had always been a terrible hiding spot...

## CHARLOTTE PURSEY (15)

Haywood Academy, Burslem

# FAMILY DINNER

I was beyond excited prancing down the worn staircase. The paintwork was admittedly questionable, Mother never finished a job properly. Well, she certainly wouldn't now. Then there are the sisters, very opinionated and never failing to revive a dead atmosphere. This time was the same, both were overly salty at the table that night. No family is complete without Dad. He's such a sweet, tender specimen, more than I had anticipated. Papa was always the one with the greatest surprises! Even then. All in all, they made a delicious meal. Now all I needed was red paint.

## ELISHA LOUISE HALL (15)

Haywood Academy, Burslem

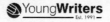
# NO

*Creak!* went the old, iron gates as Timmy pulled them ajar. He liked to explore places, and he had to go into this house. It had too many stories surrounding it. There was a note on the gate, though. It read: 'No'. Timmy still carried on. When he got to the main doors, a mysterious red message: 'No' caught his eye. Blood? He had no idea. When he opened the doors, which were surprisingly well-oiled, a breeze caught him by surprise. It came from inside the house. The gust seemed to whisper something. 'No.' And then the doors slammed shut...

BENJAMIN WARE (14)

Haywood Academy, Burslem

# THE NOISES

*Creak*. Floorboards above him made the faintest sounds. He carried on with his work. *Creak*. The sounds got louder as if they were closer. What could these mysterious sounds be? He heard a voice singing, through the baby monitor, just like his wife's. He smiled and continued with his work. Silence. Suddenly, his baby started crying loudly, before he had the chance to go and comfort her, there was a knock at the door. He edged slowly towards it. It was forced open by the wind and there was his wife. He ran upstairs...She was fast asleep.

## CHLOE RHODES (14)

Haywood Academy, Burslem

# THE TERRIFYING SCREAMS

Walking past the spine-chilling house just gave everyone the creeps. There was a thud. Everyone turned their heads the opposite way, not long after terrifying screams of a little girl came from in the house. We sprinted inside to check who the screams were coming from. It was empty no furniture, nothing... We looked around, up, and there was one room left we all went in. *Slam!* The door was slammed shut were trapped! We were all screaming for help and it never came. There was a strange man walking towards us all he snatched everyone... except me!

CARLOS MARCHESE (12)

Haywood Academy, Burslem

# THAT NIGHT...

It was midnight, dark and stormy, and I was in my living room watching TV with my lights out. Suddenly, I heard a noise, a knocking on my window, I checked and I couldn't believe my eyes... it was a terrifying, zombie-looking man, standing outside my window, glaring into my soul, holding a knife with blood dripping from it. I was in shock; I froze. The creature looked at me again. I thought I was imagining, so I closed the curtains, and checked again... it... wasn't... there. A chill went down my spine. I was terrified, shocked, and very unsafe.

## NUSRAT LEETON (13)

Haywood Academy, Burslem

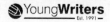

# THE CAMERA

Must and lavender hit me like a slap as I gingerly opened the charity shop door. Floorboards creaked as we glanced at the shelves; each was filled with an array of items but one stood out: a neglected camera. In my hand, it was a brick and my fingers lingered on the button - should I do it? Without further hesitation, I pressed my finger against it, mesmerized by the flash of pixels. Flicking through the recent images, harrowing sights sent chills down my spine. Suddenly, I realised the woman in the photos was my mother...who'd died 10 years ago.

KEIRA STAMP (14)

Haywood Academy, Burslem

# THE DEER

There was a deer.

No, that wasn't quite right. In fact, it wasn't a deer at all -
held no clear likeness to one. But it was a deer, for what
else could it be?

You look closer, ignoring the warning signs.

Long, spindly, disproportionate limbs, and a cracked skull
for a head - human? Deer?

Soft, human hands, that clearly resemble your own.

The screeching, crying of the souls it had eaten... stolen...

You look away, unable to comprehend more.

The deer is gone.

Your face stares back at you, and it smiles.

You should've left the deer alone.

EMMA WILLIAMS (14)

Haywood Academy, Burslem

# DARKNESS SURROUNDS

Stepping into the unknown, I was surrounded by dense, opaque fog that slowly inched in as if it were a predator ready to pounce. Suddenly from nowhere in the gloom of the night a shadow emerged! The reason it was petrifying was because soon after came a demonic laugh followed by a blood-curdling scream. I felt my heart skip a beat and I quickly started to run in a random direction watching the trees dance as I ran to safety. Or so I thought? Unfortunately, I suddenly ceased, breathless to see some sort of creature's shadow looming towards me!

USAAM ARFAN (12)

Haywood Academy, Burslem

# Breakfast Is Served

The clouds spat heavy droplets of rain attacking my skin like acid. Having enough of Mother Nature's wrath I returned home from my jog, legs sore, hands numb; head thumping vigorously. The door was wide open. But with urgency to escape the punishing weather I disregarded it - blaming the wind for this obscurity as I stumbled in. The sun hadn't yet risen, making it difficult to search for the light switch. Feeling across the room I tripped upon a wide bag, I looked down at what appeared to be a still, child-like figure. Somebody knows.

## Suhayla Bint-Ahmed (15)

Haywood Academy, Burslem

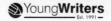

# ROOM 666

Exhausted, the man unlocked the door to Room 666. Inside: a knackered bed, a wooden rocking chair and paint peeling off the wall like dead skin. Later, the man dragged himself to the derelict bathroom, where he noticed a shadow in the corner of the mirror, but avoided it. Lights flickering, the man hauled himself into bed. He laid awake, haunted by whispers in the walls. Suddenly, the lock of the door closed, but the man was too drained to notice. A figure began to dart towards him. Screams filled the room. The man was never seen again.

ZOE JACKSON (14)

Haywood Academy, Burslem

# TRUTH OR DARE?

I was messing around with my friends, in the rain. The road was derelict. We sat around in a circle and decided to play truth or dare and I decided to ask my girlfriend, "Truth or Dare?"

She laughed, "Dare!"

I whispered into her ear, "I dare you to go into that house." And pointed at the closest house. She got up and walked towards the door. Then opened the old, creaky door and stepped in. The rest of us slammed the door on her, jokingly. We heard a deafening scream, and no one saw or heard of her again.

## KADY POVEY (11)

Haywood Academy, Burslem

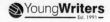
# Possessed

It was a normal night or so it seemed. Her parents had left her alone with her little sister like any other Saturday, only this one seemed different. It seemed aberrant. Twisted. Her sister seemed touchier than ever. Every word that she spoke seemed to twang with a sense of impending doom. It came to 9 o'clock and she felt a great contentment to finally put her sister to bed. There was a growling sound. She walked in to check on her sister and found her sitting up and her eyes white over. Possessed. She closed the door and ran!

## Louisa Durber (15)
Haywood Academy, Burslem

# THE ANTIQUE DOLL SHOP

Six teenage boys entered the shop. I watched closely as I'd never seen anyone come out of the antique doll shop in the village. They were there to cause trouble as I'd imagined, the little old lady slammed her fists on the desk. They laughed. She ventured into the back, the boys still laughing and mimicking her. Suddenly, the shop went completely pitch-black. I peered in. The lights came on and six dolls, identical to the teenage boys, lay scattered over the floor. She smiled and placed them on the shelf. My heart dropped.

## CHARIS HARGREAVES (13)

Haywood Academy, Burslem

# MONSTERS

Monsters are things we imagine as a child, the thing that lurks under our beds, the things that make bumps in the night, the thing that lives in our wardrobe. I think indifferently to that now, monsters usually have big teeth, wild eyes and horns. I think indifferently to that now, my wife knows that, as she lays at peace within our bedroom. I know now that monsters don't need to look like that to be monsters, they can look normal. They can walk past you all the time, now it seems, I'm staring at one in my bathroom mirror.

## GRACE SHEPHERD (15)

Haywood Academy, Burslem

# THE INVISIBLE BEAST

I can hear it. It's outside. What should I do? It comes back every night and haunts me, meets me in my dreams, and turns them into nightmares. I'm scared and alone, it's whispering, I think it's some sort of ghost or even a demon, I'm not sure but I know it's evil. The person that lived in this house before me got murdered but the police never found out who did it. I don't think it was a human that killed her, I think it was the same thing that is haunting me. It is in my room... "Help!"

JESSICA JOLLEY (12)

Haywood Academy, Burslem

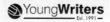

# IT IS HERE

Darkness. All I saw was darkness. I came to a house,
finally, shelter! The patio creaked and the door squealed as
it opened. Step by step, I inched closer and closer to it.
Back then, I didn't know what it was, but I was so close. Too
close. The aroma was horrid, rotting flesh? So many doors,
yet I picked that door. Why that door? *Tick-tock* went the
clock that led to my doom. My mouth felt like it had been
filled with blood. Mind tricks, I think?! That door opened. It
looked intriguing. It is here. It is me.

LUCY OSBORNE (12)

Haywood Academy, Burslem

# THE SPIRIT WITH THE AXE

I had the role of a cameraman on a show where a brave man named David Leobre went into haunted areas and sniffed out any supernatural history like a dog sniffing a scent. One day, we went into a haunted castle hearing rumours about a spirit whose famous with an axe and was called "The Spirit With The Axe." We were inside the castle and all of a sudden I heard a slash. As we turned our heads we could see a doll's head chopped off with a silhouette of a lumberjack. We never entered the castle of death again.

## JACK MILLS (15)
Haywood Academy, Burslem

# MAN IN THE MIRROR

I approached the mirror, in my attic. It had always been left there, for I had no use for it. But now, I needed it for my bedroom. It was a nice mirror, I had to admit that, but something was... Unsettling about it. Maybe it was the old, dusty frame that contained it, maybe it was that the figure reflected never seemed to match your movements. Whatever it was, it was creepy, but nevertheless, I needed it right now. I looked into it, to clean off any dust. The figure's hands reached out, grabbing my neck firmly.

## CHEYENNE KIME-LAWTON (13)

Haywood Academy, Burslem

# THE ATTIC

Our attic has never been used or seen, but today was my chance. I had an old flashlight that I could use to see up there. My father had left his ladder near the attic which I could use to climb up to it. I crept towards what could be my impending doom. Slowly, I climbed up the ladder and opened the hatch. It creaked loudly as nobody had ever used it. I walked up the ladder and reached the attic. It was extremely dusty and thick with cobwebs. Suddenly, I heard a voice behind me, but everyone was asleep...

JESSICA PAIGE SPICER (12)
Haywood Academy, Burslem

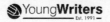

# WHAT LURKED IN THE FARM

I felt as though I was walking for months. My legs and head were heavy. The light of day that shielded me from whatever approached me, had vanished. I felt sicker by the second. I needed to rest. A small red barn caught my eye and I approached it. I tried poking the rusty padlock with a thin stick. It didn't budge. Suddenly, the hair on my neck stood on end. I turned around. Nothing there. I turned back around to see the barn door was open. I peered inside to see the figure of a troubled old lady...

## SAM BEATTIE (14)

Haywood Academy, Burslem

# THE MYSTERIOUS HOUSE

It had always been a strange house, where strange things happened in the night. But one night in the winter, a man was possessed and was urged from the demon's spirit to kill his family that were living there at the time. When everyone fell asleep, he stayed awake and snuck into each of the family member's bedrooms. One by one, he had slain them all, no one was in the house except for him and the dead bodies that lay on the floor in each room they were in. No one has seen him since that day.

LEWIS MAXFIELD (11)

Haywood Academy, Burslem

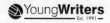
# THE UNKNOWN NUMBER

Dear Diary,

Today, I awoke, believing that it was going to be a normal day, but it was far from it. I received a message from an unknown number at around midday, telling me to meet them in this place, notorious for being eerie. I arrived there hesitantly at the agreed time, 8pm. It was silent as I pulled in across the road. As I walked into the house, I found that the door was ajar and the lights were on. All I could hear was a scream. Or all that he could hear, should I say. I'm sorry. X

## MIA HOWARD (13)

Haywood Academy, Burslem

# HELP! HELP!

As I walked past the forest I heard someone screaming, I paused. I decided to investigate. It was soon going to be night-time, so I had to hurry up. I walked into the creepy forest and it was dark so I turned my phone on so I could see what was ahead of me. The screaming came closer. I wanted to run out of there, but I thought someone could be needing my help right now. It started to rain heavily. I ran as fast as I could so I could head home. *Boom!* I fell into a never-ending hole...

ZONAIRA AKBAR (12)

Haywood Academy, Burslem

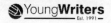

# My Deceased Heart

Silence. I wake up, looking around. It's the same old hospital room that I have been in for the past 18 years except the heart monitor has stopped. I see nurses rushing in, using the defibrillator on my lifeless body, trying to bring me back to life. Am I dead? Is it a dream? I attempt to stand up but as I look down my body is still lying on the hospital bed, petrified I look at my see-through hands and see that I am dead. Next thing I know I am getting pulled into the void...

Vinaz Maran Sadik (14)

Haywood Academy, Burslem

# THE MAN OF STONE

It was a nice sunny day until the accident. That day I let my little sister play in the forest by the park. That was a mistake. Suddenly, I heard a scream coming from the forest so I ran in to see if my sister was okay. I looked around and saw something weird. There was a statue that looked exactly like my sister but someone had smashed the head off. I walked further into the forest and saw a dark figure. Suddenly, I was unable to move. I looked at my body too had turned to stone.

OLLIE MARTIN (12)
Haywood Academy, Burslem

# Zombie Attack

I ran as fast as I could. They were catching up to me and fast. Out of the corner of my eye, I could see zombies coming after me. They were getting faster and I was getting weaker. I could feel my legs getting more tired and my mouth was dry. They began to surround me. I looked around me to see if there was a way out. There was no way. I was trapped. Exhausted, I collapsed to the ground as one approached me, as I heard a bang and the zombie fell then a human loomed over me...

## Lucy Glover (12)
Haywood Academy, Burslem

# THE STRANGER

Staying over at my friend's house, my sleep was disturbed by a lucid dream: a stranger was outside the house with an intense grin on her face, she then entered through the window and crawled around the bed. Then she stood up in the corner of the room, behind the door, and opened it so she was concealed in the darkness. I closed my eyes and counted to three. I opened them and she wasn't there. I went to wake my friend up but she rolled over and it was the woman.

LAUREN GUDERIS (14)

Haywood Academy, Burslem

# SHIVER

On a dark, stormy night, Sophie was driving but then *brum,* the car broke down. She was in the middle of a gloomy wood that had evil whispers running through it. Even though it was scary she decided to walk through to find some civilisation. Suddenly she heard someone lurking in the woods, as he slowly approached her she shivered with fear. "Come with me, I'll save you," the mysterious man said; so she followed. As she entered the castle's grand hall his fangs flashed in the candlelight and at that point, she knew she would never return home again.

## DEXTER TOWNSEND (11)

Millfield Preparatory School, Glastonbury

# THE DEATH SHOW

As I stepped out into the gloomy haze, icy fingers convulsed my arm. Dispirited statues of the wood were melancholy and alien. I felt the sharpness of dagger-like nails with a slimy substance smearing my arm. I could feel the glacial breath of a sycophantic creature on my neck; sucking up my scent. Then abruptly I heard a terrified shrill in the distance and then this violent, piercing agony overwhelmed me. Instantaneously, I heard a cackle, an immoral laugh as the creature behind me divulged its face. Heroes win battles but lose something else...

## EVA LAWSON (12)

Millfield Preparatory School, Glastonbury

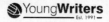
# THE CROW

The crow flew in the gloomy sky. As lightning struck the crow landed on a dark, splintered, wooden house where a man slept. It tapped on the window: *tap tap tap*. The man woke in horror; he was covered in as much sweat as a tsunami and his teeth chattered as if he were in the Arctic. He could not get back to sleep. Suddenly there was a "Boo!" from his bedside. He screamed as this shadow stood up. The man saw a glint of a knife in the shadow's hand then felt a striking pain. He went cold.

## DANIEL PEARCE (12)

Millfield Preparatory School, Glastonbury

# The Abandoned House

It was a cold night, the full moon was like a light bulb in the sky. I looked out of my window to the abandoned house up on the hill. I noticed a light flick on inside and my heart gave a leap. All I could see were two shadows, then, a man stood in the doorway holding a lantern. He hobbled down the hill, keeping to the shadows made by the trees, their branches dancing in the gentle breeze. This was my worst nightmare. He slowly sneaked down to our street. There was a knock at the door... *Bang!*

## Daniel Blight (12)

Millfield Preparatory School, Glastonbury

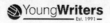

# BEHIND MY DOOR

It was the night after Halloween, my parents weren't in and something didn't feel right. It felt like someone was watching me. I heard a noise coming from behind my door, at first I didn't know what it was, but then it became louder. It was a scratching noise outside my door. At first I thought it was my dog, but then it hit me, my dog was away with my parents. At this point, I knew it was bad. I didn't know what was outside of my room, and to be honest - I didn't want to know...

TILLY ANDERTON (12)
Millfield Preparatory School, Glastonbury

# MIDNIGHT

Midnight. I couldn't sleep... I wanted to, but the feeling... someone watching me... In the corner? In my closet? Behind me? Rain pouring down. Branches attacking with rage and agony. I felt a strange fear. Eerie creaks from behind my locked door. My mind screamed in terror. Footsteps. I slowly got out of bed... walked to my dresser... slowly pushed it towards the door. *Knock-knock*. I stopped. Tears down my pale cheeks. Heart pounding. *Knock-knock*... Louder. Faster. Then excruciating silence. I released a quiet breath and... That's when I realised... whatever it was... was already behind me...

BORYS STACHOWICZ
Northfleet Technology College, Northfleet

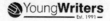
# THE CUPBOARD

Was it a hallucination caused by a fear of the dark?
I was asked to get some stationery by my teacher. Some
photocopier paper. I walked into the large cupboard, the
door slammed shut. The other lad already in there jumped.
He said his name was Doug. We both started banging on
the door and yelling, but nobody answered. The room
started to darken. Why was it getting dark? Doug said the
dark scared him to death. The door finally opened, the room
lit up, my teacher had heard me yelling. I glanced behind as
Doug walked through the wall.

## GARRY CUNNINGHAM (15)

Northfleet Technology College, Northfleet

# THE NIGHTMARE

It was the night before Halloween. "Goodnight, Frankie," said Harry, Frankie's younger brother. She climbed into her cosy, warm bed, not knowing which dreams were about to unfold... She fell asleep. Nothing happened for the first few seconds, but after a moment, the nightmare began. During the nightmare, Frankie and her friend, Tia, were both dressed in Halloween attire. They walked up to a supposedly haunted house. As they were walking up to it, Frankie accidentally scratched her finger against a nail upon the wooden door.

She awoke. She checked her finger, and there it was... The scar.

JANELLE ALLISON (12)
Oakgrove School, Middleton

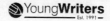

# SPINE-CHILLERS

It hovered in the air as light as feather. An eerie glow
radiating from the silhouette. I just stared unable to move as
if I was in a trance. Locked into the ground beneath my feet.
I only heard silence. Until it spoke. Chills ran down my
spine. I wanted to run but I didn't. I just stared, stared into
what I now call 'The Abyss'...

## NATASHA YALLOP (14)

Oakgrove School, Middleton

# JEORGE

He's not answering. I've been texting without any luck, too. Was he still coming?
I stop trying to call, seeing that it's nearly midnight now. Still two hours before my boyfriend thinks I'm off work and need to be picked up. And here I thought we got lucky tonight but obviously not. I take a breath, go back indoors to hear music pounding out, shaking the glasses on the bar side, customers laughing drunk probably. Wish I had the money and mates too. Two people walked in shouting. He was walking towards me with something trickling down his arm... blood...

## DAMION KNIBBS (13)
Ormiston Denes Academy, Lowestoft

# ZOMBIE

Crimson gore trickles from her flaky scalp. Clumps of expired locks perch on the ashen flooring, resting alongside a few dismantled fleshy organs. Not a beat of a heart is in vision, only a hungry glare from the pupil of a mashed eye and a sickening smirk, smiling with decayed grub-ridden fangs. Humanity diminishing, a dwindling compassion for a mortal says hello! Her beam widens with pleasure, her eyeball bulges from its socket. A crippling scent of a warm body radiates her cold soul. Another victim to feast upon. Why don't you join her, she is just a zombie!

MIA MIRGAUX (13)

Ormiston Denes Academy, Lowestoft

# THE SKYDIVE

It was a dark, scary and frightful night in the middle of what seems to be the woods. I have been stuck in here for what seems like months. What happened was that I was skydiving and I accidentally landed in here. The only thing keeping me sheltered was the parachute above me. This was one of the scariest things that had ever happened to me. I heard wolves and other creatures. *Oh no!* There were two eyes staring at me from out of the bushes. Should I run? Should I hide? Would I get out of here alive?

BETHANY HANNANT (12)
Ormiston Denes Academy, Lowestoft

# PLANE CRASH ON DESERTED ISLAND

Stranded in a wood, in a suit with a mini vodka bottle nearly empty. He laid there a bit longer until the rustling in the leaves came closer...

10 started to panic...

9 heart pounded heavily...

8 thinks, *is this the end?*

7 it was getting closer...

6 the leaves got louder...

5 heard screams...

4 an image got closer...

3 tried to move away...

2 saw a foot....

1 gasped for air... *it's here!*

A smallish cat came by, went further into the wood, as he got up he saw a light and went towards it.

## THOMAS ANNAKIN (11)

Outwood Academy Danum, Doncaster

# THE KILLING

She found herself in the middle of nowhere and suddenly stumbled across an old cabin. Reluctantly she approached the abandoned cabin and opened the door. "Argh!" She heard someone scream.

"Hello is anyone there?" she asked. There was silence. She continued walking but fell over something... It was a dead body! "Argh!" she screamed.

Out of nowhere, a mysterious figure said, "Your turn," and a psychotic grin appeared on their face. She immediately ran for the door but the person grabbed her shoulders and dragged her into the kitchen then slit her throat, blood poured everywhere...

*Will you be next?*

## SCARLETT BYRNE (13)

Outwood Academy Danum, Doncaster

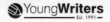

# KILLER FRIEND

"Jorden, truth or dare?" Bella whispered in a scary tone.
"Dare?" Jorden said in her usual scared tone.
"I dare you to stay a night in the murderer's house."
As Jorden walked inside the house her spine tingled with fear, Bella's eyes darted straight towards a gold box. Jorden hesitated but Bella opened it without a thought, a ghastly figure appeared for a second and possessed Bella. Bella turned towards Jorden, eyes cold. Bella picked up the nearest object, a pair of old-fashioned barber scissors, and stabbed her. Jorden fell backwards hitting her head on the wooden cupboard.

## HANNAH ROBERTS (13)
Outwood Academy Danum, Doncaster

# Happy Birthday

Alex gave her parents a 'look'. They'd organised a birthday party; there was no family there... just them. They soon left, she heard peculiar cries somewhere in the room. She studied her surroundings only to see a shadow in the radiance. She wondered what was happening, the shape stood before her... It became explicit at that moment that this was no party. She collapsed, her mind urging her to go to the door. Yet. She didn't make it... Suddenly, she witnessed the true meaning of darkness. Her mum arrived, she had a grin on her face.
"Did you have fun?"

## Aymaan Khurram (14)
Outwood Academy Danum, Doncaster

# HUNTED

*Run, just keep running,* she thought. All she heard was the wind whistling through the trees and footsteps behind. She tripped over a twisted tree root. Everything was silent. She turned around. The bright glistening moon was shining on him. He was tall and skinny. "There's no getting away now, is there child?" he whispered. He grabbed her shoulder so strongly, she couldn't help but scream, because of the pain. The next thing she knew was that she had a big bag over her head and he was dragging her across the cold, snowy ground of the dark, creepy forest...

## JESSICA NOORANY (12)

Outwood Academy Danum, Doncaster

# THE DARKNESS

Sunset was only a minute ago but the darkness was already creeping along the deserted streets, covering all the light it could find. Everyone was safe inside, away from the criminals waiting for the perfect time to pounce on an unsuspecting soul. Everyone except me. I watched the last window being consumed by the darkness. One lamppost was still on. I ran to it but I knew it was a mistake. Dark figures circled me like a pack of hyenas, waiting. I didn't know what they were waiting for until, *click*, the lamppost turned off and I was no more.

## POPPY REARDON (14)

Outwood Academy Danum, Doncaster

# HAUNTED HOUSE

It stood towering over us making us feel like an ant next to a skyscraper. As we stepped closer, the doors of the house swung open but all that could be seen was a silhouette of a person. Cautiously, we stepped inside. The floorboards creaked below our feet and every small noise was echoed throughout the house. Above us, the staircase spiralled upwards like vines on a tree. Voices echoed in my head and I felt like I was being watched. Scratches covered the walls and cracks in the floor made it feel unsteady. Suddenly, a scream came from upstairs...

## SCARLETT ROLLINSON (14)
Outwood Academy Danum, Doncaster

# THE HOUSE

The door swung open. The house looked no different, the blue walls had faded and so had the floors. But it was still home. I made my way up the stairs, to his room. A strange, eerie feeling encircled my body. On his bed sat his favourite teddy, Boris. Fear hit me as I realised that I'd taken that with me before we'd left. I turned and he was standing there watching me. "You left me."

I could hear the pain in his voice, this wasn't the boy I knew. He began to cry, not tears. Blood. "I'm so sorry."

## ELLISON SMITH (14)

Outwood Academy Danum, Doncaster

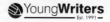
# THE FOLLOWED

They were coming. I pinched myself. Was this really real? I had to get to the police station, for I was the only witness. Nobody would believe me, of course, but it was worth a shot. I tried to recall the night's events, but they were blurry. It was a haze of deceit and death and I just wanted to forget it all. I jumped off the tube at Piccadilly and ran. I could sense that they were following me. I got to the police station, opened the door and…

"Hello," said a voice behind me. I screamed bloody murder.

## WILLIAM BATES (12)

Outwood Academy Danum, Doncaster

# Spine-Chillers

You walk down by an abandoned building, see the gates open so you enter. Turning on the flashlight and walking upon the cracking stairs as lighting hits really loud and turns off your flashlight for a second. You walk through a hall of open doors and hear somebody scream! You walk through to investigate, you feel like you are being watched. Then you find an attic, climb a ladder, there are a lot of spiders on the webs, you see a closed wardrobe, you are rapidly trembling, scared to open it. You walk up, open it then a shadow jumps...

## Jakub Kowalewski (13)
Outwood Academy Danum, Doncaster

# THE ABANDONED MANSION

I arrived in front of the creepy, abandoned mansion and walked through the massive, rotten doors, I stopped. It was silent. The door creaked and suddenly closed. The wind blew through the broken windows and I got goosebumps when I saw the dry blood on the shards of glass from the filthy floor. I froze when I saw the light flickering and heard a scream that stopped my next actions. The scream came from the ceiling. I went up the old spiral stairs and headed to the only open door. I opened the door and let out a loud screech...

GEORGIANA UNGUREANU (13)

Outwood Academy Danum, Doncaster

# THE DARK MANSION

As you approach the rotten gate to the haunted manor, it opens with a loud creak. Slowly, after you hear what you think to be a scream, you rush in through the crooked, old door to investigate. Then you smell something rotten and cover your face with the collar on your shirt as you move towards the stairs. Then the door closes behind you, you hear the scream again although this time it's closer. Even so, you man up and brave the long walk up the creaky, rotten stairs. When you reach the top you get a big surprise…

OWEN BUNDAY (11)

Outwood Academy Danum, Doncaster

# THE ONE-EYED MONSTER

There I was, walking down the hallway. Silence. A shining glimpse of what I thought to be a flashlight turned out to be a one-eyed creature. Darkness... *What is going on?* I thought. Rushing to find the exit, the adrenaline was kicking in. I had a feeling I was alone or was I..? I could feel my legs shaking, I knew I wasn't alone, I had the feeling in my heart, which felt like it was breaking. Finally, I could see the precious exit sign, I ran up to it but the door suddenly shut. It was over for me...

## IOANA GONGEANU (11)

Outwood Academy Danum, Doncaster

# No Escape

Everything was dark, quiet, the candle suddenly blew out! I attempted to escape, running to the door I heard creeping upstairs, I decided to look, the stairs creaked like they were a hundred years old, I had definitely lost the element of surprise. I could hear my heart beating in my chest, I paused to calm myself, then I saw it! It was out of my nightmares, it had no eyes, yet it came towards me like it knew I was there, it was like it could smell fear. I stopped breathing, but I knew there was no escape.

## Jack Brookes (12)
Outwood Academy Danum, Doncaster

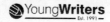

# THE UNEXPLAINABLE BOOK

As I step through an utterly wrecked door, I reach for a dusty antique book on a broken bookshelf. This particular book had *'read me if you dare'* written on the cover of the book. For a second I hesitate to read it. The voice inside of me tells me to stop, put the book down and get out of there at once, however, I still somewhat have the urge to read the bizarre-looking book. I hold it in my hands and gaze at its ancient, time-worn cover. I flip over the cover and there it is…

BELIZ ERDOGDU (13)
Outwood Academy Danum, Doncaster

# THE LADY IN THE WINDOW

As I was halfway to Mum's house, a heavy storm had rolled over the motorway and it was dark with no street lights. Out of the blue, a doe jumped in front of the car, I swerved off of the road and knocked myself out. As I groggily and gradually awoke, I noticed that I could not move and I could hear a quiet humming. I looked across and saw a massive house and in one of the windows was a dim light. But it started to get brighter. Just as it got blinding a waving woman crept into view...

HAYDEN HORNE (12)
Outwood Academy Danum, Doncaster

# Spine-Chiller

As she walks through the old, abandoned safe house, she hears movement close by and grips her knife tighter. The figure jumps at her from behind, spinning around, she cuts into the feeble fabric, slicing into his skin, the blood splatters onto her already bloody clothes. He falls to the ground trying to escape, more blood spilling into the cracks of the floor, begging her to spare his life. Silence fills the house once more as she continues her search for more victims, cleaning the bloody blade with her tongue. "This is all for you my love," she mutters.

## Abbie Dixon
Ramsey Grammar School, Isle Of Man

# THE DOLL

Eyes locked on the old, ramshackle shop, which laid among the lonely streets packed with thick, gleaming snow. The door creaked with gusts of the winter's breeze barging in, she followed... It was there...Staring right into her. *Dolls are just dolls, right?* she thought... Lowering her senses, strolling toward the ragged doll, something wasn't right, familiar. Identical to the one she cuddles and comforts! *How did it get here?* Her hands slipped through its ruffled locks, with a shiver. Laid on the floor. And the shelf... She's a doll, on a shelf, betrayed by the one she loved most.

## MIRREN ELWICK (12)
Scalby School, Newby

# A Blood-Curdling Coaster

The mist surrounded me as the darkness swirled to create an infinite black hole swallowing the abandoned theme park. "Sam?" I called, though no answer. The park was eerily still. As I looked back to leave, a menacing, disembodied voice slithered into my ear.

"Harry."

I stopped dead. The howl of the wind whistled through the forsaken rides. As I slowly turned on my feet, the trees watched my every move, a ghostly figure stood solitary in the shadows.

Terror-stricken I called, "Sam... is that you?" I felt a squalid hand touch my shoulder and my muscles turned to ice.

## Louis Fell (12)
Scalby School, Newby

# THE WOODS

I descended into the deep woods for my walk. The vivid sun setting, the sky painted deep red. I usually liked this walk, secluded and peaceful. Not tonight. First noticing the jaggedness of the branches and dishevelled leaves lying lifelessly. Howling wind darting between trees. The further, the darker. The usual breeze and birds had gone. Deadly silent. Tried to stay calm, something eerily different. Finally reaching the campfire it's never used because only I come here. I would now turn around but I noticed the campfire smouldering, then a twig snapped behind me, I realised I was not alone.

EVIE WARDELL (15)
Scalby School, Newby

# Away From The Storm

It is dark and the rain is heavy, lightning strikes and the night sky lights up. *Find shelter,* I think. I run to the building in the distance it seems abandoned. That's exactly why I don't want to venture inside. Lightning strikes again and scares me inside. The building seems desolate, further in I hear rustling. I catch a glimpse of something scurrying away. "Just a cat," I tell myself, this place is raising questions. Finding a place to rest, I curl up and sleep. After falling into dreams, I'm awakened by a bony hand on my shoulder...

## Zachary Parker (12)

Scalby School, Newby

# PUPPET MASTER

I couldn't hide, couldn't run. My feet, frozen and numb, refusing movement, surrendering to the ravenous jaws of death crawling through my body, gnawing away at my feeble soul. My mind screamed agonisingly, drowning in an ocean of despair; I felt my body go under, water piling into my throat, choking me until all life was drained from my tragic body. My blood ran stone-cold. My eyes bulged to the brim of their sockets. And I saw him. Standing there. Controlling me. I collapsed into the ground. It was done. I was his powerless puppet, he my murderous master.

## EMILY GASKELL (11)
Scalby School, Newby

# THE LOST TRAIN

She's guarding its blue body, its face scratched black, tears of blood racing down its face.

I sat upright in a sweat. I launched out of bed, put my shoes on and fled to the forbidden forest. The trees looked down on me, their roots climbing towards me, the moon full, at that moment, I heard a… whistle?

I followed the sound… it couldn't be. There were no tracks. I edged closer to the machine. I saw… a girl with blood down her face. I asked if she wanted to come home with me. She said, "You're not going home."

## KAITLYN JAYDE BYRAM (12)
Scalby School, Newby

# THE ASYLUM

One night, it was just for one night... He would sleep there to show his friends he wasn't a wuss then leave immediately. But as his friends grew more wild in their endeavours, he shrank away from his. As he entered the abandoned asylum, he almost felt the chilling cackles of the insane rising above him. Then he stopped... a sixth sense told him someone was behind... He felt every muscle inside of him flinch, his breath escaped in short, quick bursts. Then as his screams finally died away, the ritual could, with this last sacrifice, finally be upon them...

## KYLE ROBINSON (12)
Scalby School, Newby

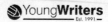

# Taxi Mayhem

The taxi driver's first call of the day was from Doris, a regular customer. The sleeve of her dress was stained red and she was be-cloaked in a long, purple scarf. As she stepped into the car, the child-lock clamped shut and the brakes released. She seemed strangely quiet and appeared to be messing with a small object partially obscured by the scarf. *Drip!* The driver turned to see a child drinking a red substance. He stopped the car abruptly and dialled 999... but by the time the police arrived all that could be found was a long, purple scarf.

## Hannah Brown (12)

Scalby School, Newby

# THE CACKLE

Oliver was lost! Running home, he found himself alone on a desolate street that he hadn't seen before, he was confused. The end house had a light glowing from an upstairs room. Oliver found himself drawn to the house and as he looked up at the window he saw frightened eyes looking back at him. Oliver gulped! He was scared but opened the front door and shouted, "Hello?" Upstairs there was a terrific bang, Oliver's adrenaline told him to get out of there quickly! He turned to run but the door had disappeared. Behind him a cackle shrieked...

## HARRISON ROEBUCK (13)
Scalby School, Newby

# WHAT'S IN THE WOODS?

Walking through the woods seemed like a brilliant idea, I've done it before. Crunching caught my attention. I spun around. There, on the path, was movement as if something was standing there. Keeping my eyes on the place I thought the thing was, I cautiously stepped backward. A low growl cut me off, the kind that sends shivers up someone's back. The invisible thing stepped forward; well I think it did. I took off running, not looking back until I was home. I still don't know what it was but since that night I have never gone in those woods.

ISOBEL PASHBY (14)
Scalby School, Newby

# TRAPPED

Help! I can't move. Hands bound, jaw clenched. An ear-splitting shriek fills my ears - I have to help them. Cold hands slither across my torso, clawing at my chest. Every passing second I get colder and colder, the cries becoming fainter and fainter. I am finished. Patterns dance before my eyes in the half-light. Is it just me or are the walls closing in tighter? The roof crushes down on my lungs, squeezing out whatever life remains in me. One last breath... This isn't real.
Harsh lights reflect off the glass of the lab wall. I'm trapped!

## AMELIE WILLIAMS (12)
Scalby School, Newby

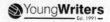

# DON'T SCREAM

It's dark and deadly silent. Lowering myself off the bed, my bare feet plant themselves on the stone-cold floor. When suddenly, a blood-curdling scream rings through the corridor. The beating of my heart fills the room alongside my heavy breaths. A figure strides past the room, pausing for a second outside my door. I find myself holding my breath, restraining from releasing a scream of my own. I watch the figure turn around searching for someone. But before I can move, their eyes locked with mine and I freeze. As a wave of fear floods me, I...

## HANNAH SELLERS-DRURY (14)

Scalby School, Newby

# THE WOODS

The sun was setting on the horizon, I had to get to shelter. I started running and heard a scream, I skidded to a stop. The scream came again desperate and afraid. Adrenaline shot through me like a hot poker. I couldn't leave her, not this time. The darkness was drawing closer to me, pressing down, suffocating me slowly as I sprinted through the thick maze of woodland. I stopped and looked up at the body hanging above me, my face draining of colour. "Mom?" An icy-cold hand gripped my shoulder, and at that moment I knew I was next...

## MARYLYNN RODGER (15)
Scalby School, Newby

# LANI

The night rolled in. With nowhere but emptiness, I continued to swim. Looking around frantically, I couldn't see anything that resembled life - only the crashing sea waves. I knew it was only a matter of time before I grew tired. I strained to see land or boat or something solid to stand on. Then I remembered. Moments before it happened, I had texted Lani. She would come and find me! Miraculously, her boat appeared. My legs gave in. A hand pulled me aboard - I was on her boat. I didn't see her butterfly tattoo. This wasn't Lani.

## MATILDA BROWN (13)
Scalby School, Newby

# THE ABANDONED MANSION

We had to run into the abandoned mansion, hiding in the wardrobe. We could hear the downstairs floorboards creaking. We sat there silently, but in the inside, we knew it could be the end. We heard the loud footsteps coming closer and this crazy man opened the door to the room that we were hiding in. He started searching in our room, we heard heavy breathing as the wardrobe started to slowly open. Now we knew it was the end, and then *bang!* My dad yelled, "Found you!" and that is how we lost the game of hide-and-seek.

JACK LANGMEAD (14)
Scalby School, Newby

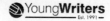

# The Window

It was the same time. The same route. The same reason.
Yet something didn't feel the same. I heard something
creaking up above. I looked up. I noticed an upstairs
window that was open in a deserted neighbouring house; it
was creaking as the breeze passed. Why was it open? It
wasn't open yesterday.

As I approached the house, the fog, that was in the
distance, surrounded my feet. The cold atmosphere held me
hostage as I entered the front garden. Clifford was cowering
between my legs as if he could sense something. What was
it?

Rose Wanless (12)
Scalby School, Newby

# THE PENSIONER, THE NURSE AND THE IMPOSTER

Like any usual day, I entered my grandad's room in his care home. Although today I noticed he was sleeping, so I sat down on a plush, red seat and waited. It was then that I heard a murmur and looked up to see him sleep-talking. Firstly, it sounded like, "Ehhhhh" but as it got louder it was, "He will come!" Then freakishly he screamed a high-pitched, blood-curdling scream. I thought he was in pain so I ran to get a nurse. The nurse explained that he had left the building hours ago. So who was in the bed?

LUCY BROWN (12)
Scalby School, Newby

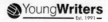

# Nocturnal

Fog was creeping in. I wouldn't make it back before dawn or before the sky turned to darkness. Waiting for Mum to come in the thick fog seemed a good idea, but waiting in an old, derelict church didn't. The door was unlocked so I walked in. In the old, broken, rundown church I sat down on an unused chair. I then turned my head to look to the left and saw that every single painting had eyes staring right at *me...* Who was there? As I waited for Mum I heard floorboards creaking and strange noises! Was I alone?

## Harriet Benson (12)
Scalby School, Newby

# THE FALL

I was dangling. I could feel the grip getting looser. The gravel in the cave shifted. I could hear the strange breathing of whatever was holding me. Suddenly, the thing let go of my ankle. I was descending into the pit of stalagmites. Even though I would surely die, I was strangely not scared. The icy air whizzed in my face. I could now see the bottom. I braced myself as I saw the spike mercilessly pierce my chest. That split second of pain was my last experience. The blood drained from my body. Was I the first to fall?

STAN VICKERS (12)
Scalby School, Newby

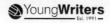

# THE STORY OF A FAMILY WHO JUST WANTED TO GO FOR A WALK

In the evening of a Sunday, a family decided to go for a walk through a haunted forest thinking it was a good idea. The forest had been haunted for the past decade. They were 2 miles into the forest with the entrance nowhere in sight. They were lost. Suddenly they heard a scream. They ran towards it and when they got there, they saw an old army bunker that had been abandoned. Then the scream again, coming from inside. The dad went inside, then the two sons then mother. That family was never seen again...

## THOMAS JEY (12)
Scalby School, Newby

# Scary Story

A shack lay on a hill that looked like a breath could break it. Inside, a family was sleeping. Suddenly there was a bang at the door. The young boy woke, crept to the top of the stairs and peered through the railings. The creaky door opened, and a big bald man stood there with a bag. He dropped the bag and out rolled two pale heads! Instantly the boy knew the heads were his parents' heads! The boy stared and sniffed, suddenly the man looked at the boy with fully white eyes and a snake-like tongue...

## Jack Parkes (13)
Scalby School, Newby

# THE HOUSE

Here we were. The abandoned house. As my sister and I snuck into the small, dark cottage, we heard something. I peeped my head around the corner and saw the silhouette of what looked like a young girl. She was singing beautifully, although something wasn't right. She had long dark hair and was wearing a red dress. The figure suddenly turned towards us, her face horribly disfigured. We ran as fast as we could. Once we were out of sight, we sat down and both agreed never to speak of what we saw again.

LIANA MORE (12)
Scalby School, Newby

# The Investigation

It was late at night, I was sent to investigate an asylum with Officer Wilson. We got to the front door. It was cold, fog curled the asylum like crows at a graveyard. The door opened with a creak, and we were horrified by what we saw. A man on the floor was beheaded. Both shaking with fear, we carried on. Wilson said, "We better get a raise for this." As we walked across what seemed to be a never-ending corridor, we saw a figure, as they walked in the light, it was a man grinning ear to ear.

## Ellis Mearns (13)
Scalby School, Newby

# THE LAKE

I felt like I was being watched walking my dog along the river edge. It felt eerie. I started running but suddenly, there was a loud roar and a huge, fierce monster rose from the water. My dog bolted but the monster grabbed my body dragging me under. I was petrified! It was icy-cold and I was thrashing my body to get away but its grip was getting tighter, dragging me deeper in the river. I couldn't escape and I knew I was drowning. I screamed, sat bolt upright and realised it was all a dream!

ALFIE RACE (13)
Scalby School, Newby

# THE PURPLE SPOTS!

We are on a windy path heading to the leaf with purple spots on. It was clear at one minute but then the mist made us not able to see more than 5 metres the next. The trees were moving, making shadows that made us jump! Bill went to touch the leaf with his trembling hand, suddenly there was no sound at all. I dived in front of him so he wouldn't touch it, but I fell on it instead. I realised purple spots were appearing all over my body. In a second, I was gone!

## CHARLIE BROADHEAD (13)
Scalby School, Newby

# BEHIND THE DOOR

As I trudged through the gloomy forest in the swirling rain, I could just make out an abandoned house. At last - shelter! I decided to approach the house. When I reached the rotten, old door, I could hear strange noises coming from within. I opened the door and crept up the hardened stairs. I looked around and there was nobody in sight. Slowly, I inched back downstairs and to my horror, I noticed pictures stained with patterns of blood...

## AIDAN STOCKILL (14)
Scalby School, Newby

# WILD BOARS

*Whoosh*, the sound of the road, my first experience on a motorway. "What's that scraping sou-..."
"Mum! Dad! Wake up!"
I passed out and awoke in a stark, cold hospital ward... my parents hadn't made it.
Apparently unscathed, I was going to an orphanage called Wild Boars. The name instantly sent shivers down my spine.
Arriving, there's a sign: *Misbehaving kids? Wild Boars will sort them out.*
People wearing black suits exited buildings. When caught, they'd drown you in a bucket of worms.
And to this day I have an undigested worm rotting at the back of my throat... cough.

## CHRISTOPHER HORN (10)

Solefield School, Sevenoaks

# THE LURKER

I rose from the cabin of my ship and immediately sensed something was wrong. It was quiet. Usually the crew were bustling about and yelling 'port side' or 'starboard'. A tingling sensation rose in my stomach; I felt sick. "Hello," I yelled. No answer.

I started to get frightened; goosebumps ran up my arm. The rain patted against my face, blinding me for a second. Then I saw a figure. "Is this some sick joke?" I demanded, anger swelling inside me. Then the figure turned around, saw me, lunged a clawed hand into my leg and began to feast.

## JOSHUA EDWARDS (12)
Solefield School, Sevenoaks

# Fog

As he wandered through the marsh, Oliver wondered if this was really the best idea. His friend's voices echoed in his head: "Chicken, are you?" they had said and that had landed him here, seeking for a something that would kill everything it saw. "Only a myth," he encouraged himself. Suddenly a groan came from the water. As soon as this happened, Oliver bolted the way he had come, but fog blocked the way. He couldn't see more than a couple of inches. But Oliver didn't see the hand reach out of the fog and reach for his throat...

## Luke Edwards (12)

Solefield School, Sevenoaks

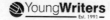
# JUST ONE MOLAR!

I woke up in a cold, mechanical chair, the dim light flickering, blurring my vision. I would have screamed, but my voice was disabled. It was almost impossible to see. However, there was one figure, hunched over next to a little table. His ghostly voice echoed in a blood-curdling tone, "Let me just get that molar out." His crooked fingers stabbed a syringe into my neck. It was beyond pain. After the injection my arms and legs stiffened. Then, as my face contorted, he plunged his sharp, shiny tools menacingly into my mouth. But then it all went red.

KINN JANSEN (11)
Solefield School, Sevenoaks

# VICTOR THE VEGAN VAMPIRE

On a stormy night, in a huge castle, a vampire named Victor was squeezing the juice out of a tomato. He was making vegan blood from a recipe in a black and white book. He needed one more ingredient, a cucumber, but whenever he went to get one, humans would throw sticks at him. *Savages!* he thought.

At dusk, he flew to the shop. What did his book say about cucumbers? 'Cylinder shaped and curved at the ends.' He found a red object that matched the description, brought the pepperoni home and finished the recipe. Delicious, but maybe not vegan?

ARTHUR MITCHELL-CLARK (11)
Solefield School, Sevenoaks

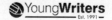

# No Hope Asylum

On a frosty winter's night, I was staring into one of the filthy bedroom windows of the haunted 'No Hope Asylum', watching them rise out of their beds, dragging their feet across the chipped stone floor, looking for food. I could hear their moans and groans become louder as they tried to smash through the ancient wooden doors. Suddenly, I felt a cold, bony hand reach for my shoulder and before I knew it, I was being dragged along the path into the asylum. My mind was racing. Am I one of them now? No one knows, no one cares.

## William Walters (11)
Solefield School, Sevenoaks

# ENTRANCED

*Pat! Pat!* The gutter was leaking onto the street. The fog was thick and dense, like ordinary, but this, this was different, in a way that no one could comprehend. I walked through it, soaked to the bone; the street was like a ghost town. Most Saturdays, I would meet up with my friends and gossip. I walked into the church; the faint murmur of hymns being sung entranced me. I was inside but the church was empty; I paused, then it stopped and was silent. *Pat! Pat!* I swung around and saw a putrefying, beastly image!

## HARRY PATERSON (12)
Solefield School, Sevenoaks

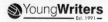

# THE BOG

A putrid smell wafted up my nose making me feel sick. The sludge below me was turning and little mosquitos buzzed around my hat. For the hundredth time, I raised my hand to try and swat away the pesky insects. Behind me, the swamp let out bubbles of horrid smelling gas. To my right, I was starting to see the rotting corpses of those who had gone before me, hunting for the very treasure I now seek.
The creatures of this bog lurked in the shadows, waiting for the right moment to pounce and devour me.
I turned around ...

FINLAY HAWKINS
Solefield School, Sevenoaks

# THE MYSTERY CASTLE

The trees were whirling from side to side. The howling wind filled the dark night sky. I was alone and my only option right now was to walk into this old, ragged castle. I knew it wasn't a good idea. I immediately tried to turn back but the doors had locked behind me. There was a sudden screech echoing round the castle. In the blink of an eye I heard a loud thump. I shone my torchlight, which, honestly, I should have done as soon as I entered the castle. But when I turned my back, everything went black.

GEORGE BROWN

Solefield School, Sevenoaks

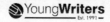
# HUNTED AND HAUNTED

The criminals were hanged, the royal force had finished their job, the hunt was over, or was it? I went to sleep that night but then heard a clatter noise. The old grandfather clock had fallen over. I went over to pick it up but I heard that clatter noise again. It was from the kitchen. Hesitantly, I went in and the kitchen had horror within. They were back; alive from the dead. They saw me and I ran away from them as far as I could go. I tripped. I fell to the ground, unconscious. Then black came...

JASPER TYM

Solefield School, Sevenoaks

# TOM AND I

The trees towered over us, like the tower of death. The gloomy fog blinded our vision. There was no escape from this agitation. Panic ran through my veins. Ravens flew over us, like a dark cloud. They were a sign; leading us to our deaths. Suddenly, I saw a shadow, waving wildly, as soulless as a ghost. All the colour drained from my skin. Tom wasn't there! "Tom?" I wailed with panic exploding from me. There was nothing but silence in reply. Silence and an empty space. Was I next? A cold, pale hand touched my shoulder. I was doomed.

KRISTIAN MICHAEL (15)
St Andrew The Apostle Greek Orthodox School, London

# ISOLATION

The soulless forest sat, in isolation. I dodged through the shadowy maze, while the obscured, tall, trees waved horrifically. I had to get home, but the dark isolated forest encircled me, leaving me hopeless. Thunder crowded round my ears. The heavens roared, wailed and moaned in despair and the wind seemed to whisper the voices of the dead. Suddenly in the still distance, a pair of bright, red eyes glared at me. It had found me. I stepped back as a stocky figure loomed out of the darkness, its eyes raging. Death had come to take me...

BEN REID (15)
St Andrew The Apostle Greek Orthodox School, London

# THE OTHER SIDE OF THE STREET

I was lurking around the depleted, deserted street. There was no sign of life. The old house stood there: looking at me, as if it was alive and breathing. I could hear a moan, which made me imagine the dead emerging from their graves. I quickly turned with caution as I saw a black shadow pass across me from above. Fear crept through me, as the inhumane eyes of a creature locked on to me from the creaky rooftop. Out of nowhere, daggers pierced right through my body, launching me against the old, burnt down walls where my fate ceased...

JASON MARVON (14)
St Andrew The Apostle Greek Orthodox School, London

# SILENCE

Silence. The eerie silence shrouded me like a blanket. Everywhere I went, there were tall trees; they all looked the same. But, I had to keep on running. Running from fear and anxiety, knowing that if I kept on running, I would be safe. Suddenly, for a split second, I thought I saw a glowing red light. Like a moth drawn to the flame, I rushed to it, hoping that it was some sort of survivor. I was getting closer and closer, step by step. Twigs snapped under me. I looked up, at what looked like hell. I gasped...

## MIA LO BUE (14)

St Andrew The Apostle Greek Orthodox School, London

# DEMON

I ran, ran as quickly as my weak legs could go. Suddenly I felt his breath creep upon my neck. I peeked round. There he was. I was defenceless; exhausted from the running and falling over. He grabbed me, and pulled me into the darkness. I tried to scream, but the more I tried, the tighter he squeezed my neck. My fear was endless. My heart was beating out of my chest. In the distance, I saw a ghostly staircase. If only I could get there, but his grip got tighter and his eyes burnt into my skin. Help me!

SIENNA TIERNEY (11)
St Andrew The Apostle Greek Orthodox School, London

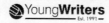

# THE DARKNESS WITHIN

As I ran through the ghostly forest, I could hear her. She looked like she was straight out of her grave. Her movements were elegant and soft, slow, deliberate. Not something that you would expect. As she got closer and closer to the light, I saw her face. It was me. I stopped. Still. What was she? How did she get here? Then she spoke, in a distorted voice, "I am not you and you are not me. I am everyone and everything you fear. There is no escape from me. I am your end."

ANNA PHOTIOU (13)

St Andrew The Apostle Greek Orthodox School, London

# INFERIORS TO THE RICH

Fallen bodies. Blood surrounding the wrinkles and crevices in their heads. Adults screaming for their lost, empty souls amidst the battle of their lives. Knives swiping shivers down spines, bows striking the hearts of the helpless and empty-eyed. Lost pulses, feelings, colour among the land of barren and deserted souls. They were there to die. At the expense of the rich. They fought and loved for their survival, whilst it was watched on the plasma screens in wealthy houses. Their pain gave mild heartache to them, leaving a family restless, broken and shaken. All because they wanted entertainment.

## LOIS KATIE HILTON (15)
St Catherine's College, Eastbourne

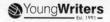
# THE SCRATCHING

The scratching on my wooden closet door comforts me. My cat's always been obscure. He always scratches on the injured door whenever he sees me distressed. He's been doing this ever since we've moved into this peculiar house. The scratching on the rusty door makes me feel like I'm not alone and he's there to protect me from any sort of danger. It's almost like he can read my mind, which is warming. Well, it used to be. It's kind of unsettling now I live alone... The man in the closet took him away. I wonder when he'll be back?

## MICHAELA REDPATH (12)
St Thomas More RC Academy, North Shields

# FROM DUST AND TO DUST YOU SHALL RETURN

The steady thump of the heart monitor reminded me that she was still alive in her pale and old skin. She was on her last legs in the hospital bed, babbling about nothing and everything. I was clutching her frail hand watching blood coursing through her veins. Suddenly, her temperature started to decline rapidly, I shouted for doctors and nurses, but no one came. Then, all the machines around her turned off abruptly. I couldn't feel her pulse. She rapidly decomposed. Now, all she was, was a pile of dust on the bed. Like she was never there at all.

## IZZY DUTTON (13)

St Thomas More RC Academy, North Shields

# THE SOUL CAPTURER

Amara's heart pulsated as she scurried through the empty car park. The mysterious soul capturer slowly creeping closer and closer, ready to make the little girl vanish from existence. She found a shortcut, so she thought, but really the soul capturer was trying to lead her that way because it led to his underground surgery. Suddenly, there was a massive puff of smoke and there Amara was tied to a metal bed, with the soul capturer leaning over her. After a couple of weeks, she was freed out to the world. No soul. No memory.

## GRACE PEDDIE (13)

St Thomas More RC Academy, North Shields

# TICK! TOCK!

I couldn't wait for my friend to come! It was three already! How long? *Ting!* Yes, finally! I opened the door excitedly, only to see or feel nothing, but a wind slapping my face! I turned red and boiled with anger! I harshly slammed the door! "No!" I roared! In a blink of an eye, the lights turned off… Everything was black! I couldn't even see a thing! My heart beat faster… *Bang!* The clock suddenly fell off but it was working; *tick-tock!* I decided not to even have a glimpse behind! Suddenly, a hand covered my eyes… "St-stop!"

TEERNA BHAUMIK (11)
The Literacy House International, Tintagel

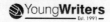
# THE DEATH BEARING SONG!

The moon shone across my face, making it hard to see. Shadows of creatures were cast down beside my trembling body. Every step I made in the fog engulfed forest, the louder the death song became. On some stones lay beautiful creatures sitting on them, the ones singing the death song. Enchanting it was...my body lost control drawing closer to them. *Snap!* A twig got smashed. The spell was broken. Instead of the beautiful creatures that laid there before, I saw grey wrinkled creatures. Those things came closer. The sun started rising. I closed my eyes. Suddenly, they disappeared!

## SAMARA NORONHA (12)

The Literacy House International, Tintagel

# Jack Out Of The Box

Warily, I drifted toward the small wooden box, braced for the patronising smile that was going to arise. I waited, but it never happened. Relief washed over me - but was cut short. Suddenly, I became aware of the scorching heat. I spun around to a flurry of scarlet and orange flames that danced tauntingly in front of the door. Panicked, I backed away only to trip over the hollow, empty box.

Glowing flames engulfed the room. Everything was on fire - except the ever-smiling face that watched me, a matchbox in hand... Jack was out of the box.

Lois Van Den Broek (13)
The Portsmouth Academy, Portsmouth

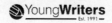
# THE ABANDONED MANSION

You walk to the old, abandoned mansion, trembling with fear. After a few minutes you build the courage and use your sweaty hand to open the creaking door. Then you are face-to-face with two more doors. Which door do you choose? After choosing a door, you walk down a dark corridor that ends with an elevator. You enter. *Screaaaam!* What was that? You try to leave but the doors slam shut. After reaching the bottom, the doors rapidly open. The first thing to catch your eye is a bleeding man cuffed to a chair...

## OAKLEY LANCETT (13)

The Portsmouth Academy, Portsmouth

# THE HOUSE DOWN THE ROAD:

*Bang!* I opened my eyes. A flash of light filled up the room. I picked up my phone and the time was 2:30am. I had an unread message from a private number. I opened it. It was an address, I was curious about where it was. Suddenly another message demanded me to go there. I saw a bright white light, by the door. I followed this light. It moved like a snowflake leading me towards an abandoned house. The door swung open with a creak. Before I saw what the house held the light turned black. Then I awoke. Alone.

## BROOKE KNIGHT (12)

The Portsmouth Academy, Portsmouth

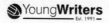

# THE GRAVEYARD

It was like every other vacation that we had been to, except this year it was strange. This place was suspicious. However, every night, my elder sister and I would go to the graveyard and we'd play hide and go seek. Until one night I saw a figure. Thinking it was my sister I went over to look, but just when I was going to look the figure stared at me longingly. At this moment, I ran whilst an arm held on to me so tight, I could not breathe... I made it out alive, but my sister was missing.

## JANNAH BUSHRA (12)
The Portsmouth Academy, Portsmouth

# Untitled

It was a dark winter's night I was house watching for my nan she was in Florida with some church friends. I was just about to go to bed then I heard a noise. "Hello," someone said in a sinister whine. I went downstairs it sounded like it was coming from the door. There was no peephole so I went to the living room
window and carefully looked so it didn't look like I was but I was greeted by the old lady with a sinister smile. It was like she knew I was going to look there...

## Charlie Payne

The Portsmouth Academy, Portsmouth

Est.1991

# YOUNG WRITERS
# INFORMATION

We hope you have enjoyed reading this book – and
that you will continue to in the coming years.

If you're a young writer who enjoys reading and creative writing, or the
parent of an enthusiastic poet or story writer, do visit our website
www.youngwriters.co.uk. Here you will find free
competitions, workshops and games, as well as
recommended reads, a poetry glossary and our blog.

If you would like to order further copies of this book, or any of our other
titles, then please give us a call or visit **www.youngwriters.co.uk.**

Young Writers
Remus House
Coltsfoot Drive
Peterborough
PE2 9BF
(01733) 890066 / 898110
**info@youngwriters.co.uk**